Walt Disney's Dumbo

Senior Designer: Elaine Lopez
Editor: Sharon Yates
Editorial Director: Pamela Pia

Walt Disney's Dumbo, copyright © 1955, 2004 Disney Enterprises, Inc.
Story adapted by Annie North Bedford. Illustrations adapted by Dick Kelsey.

C E

Walt Disney's
Dumbo

Illustrations by The Walt Disney Studios

Story adapted by Annie North Bedford
Illustrations adapted by Dick Kelsey

Reader's
Digest
Children's Books™

Pleasantville, New York • Montréal, Québec • Bath, United Kingdom

It was spring — springtime in the circus! After the long winter's rest, it was time to set out again on the open road, and everyone was eager to go.

"*Toot! Toot!*" whistled Casey Junior, the locomotive of the circus train.

"All aboard!" shouted the Ringmaster.

The acrobats, the jugglers, the tumblers, and the snake charmers scrambled to their places on the train. The keepers locked the animals' cages. Then, with a jiggety jerk and a brisk *puff-puff*, off sped Casey Junior. The circus was on its way!

TO THE CIRCUS →

Everyone was happy. All the mother animals had new babies to love. All but Mrs. Jumbo. Her baby elephant had not yet arrived, and she wondered how the stork would ever find her.

But what was this? A special-delivery stork was flying after the circus train. "Mrs. Jumbo? Where is Mrs. Jumbo?" he asked.

Eventually, the stork found the elephant car and left his precious bundle at Mrs. Jumbo's side.

All the other elephants were waiting to see the new baby. And what a darling, chubby baby elephant he was.

"Koochie-koo, little Jumbo, koochie-koo!" said one of the grown-ups as she tickled the baby under his chin.

The tickling made him sneeze. And when he sneezed, out flapped his enormous ears! The biggest ears any elephant had ever seen!

"He'll never be a little Jumbo." The grown-ups laughed. "Little Dumbo is the name for him!"

Poor little Dumbo toddled to his mother, and tenderly she rocked him to sleep in her trunk.

Before morning dawned, Casey Junior brought the train to a stop in the city where the circus was to open that day. Then the circus folk got ready for the big parade.

Down the main street pranced the gay procession. There were cream-white horses and licorice-colored seals. There were lady acrobats in pink silk tights and lions pacing in their gilded wagon-cages, and last but not least came the elephants marching slowly, in single file.

At the end of the line came little Dumbo. "Look at that silly animal with the draggy ears!" cried the crowd. "He can't be an elephant! He must be a clown!"

Dumbo, toddling along behind his mother with his trunk clasped around her tail, tried to hurry faster so he wouldn't hear the laughter. But alas, he stumbled and tripped on his ears. Down he went in a puddle of mud. The crowd roared with laughter at the baby elephant.

Back in the tent, Mrs. Jumbo gave Dumbo a bath so that he would look fine for the first show that afternoon. Then, they ate their lunch and went to their stalls in the menagerie.

Soon the crowd was streaming through the tents. A group of boys gathered near the rope in front of Mrs. Jumbo's stall. "We want to see the baby elephant!" they yelled. "The one with the sailboat ears!"

A boy grabbed one of Dumbo's ears and pulled it, hard. Then he made an ugly face and stuck out his tongue.

Mrs. Jumbo could not stand to see Dumbo being teased. She reached out with her trunk, snatched the boy up, dropped him across the rope, and spanked him.

"Help, help!" he cried. And then the keepers arrived.

Mrs. Jumbo reared on her hind legs. But soon she was behind the bars in the prison wagon with a big sign above her that said DANGER! MAD ELEPHANT! KEEP OUT!

Worst of all, the other elephants would have nothing to do with Dumbo. They even turned their backs on him in a solid wall.

Now, hidden in the hay pile was Timothy Mouse, the circus mouse. Timothy loved scaring elephants, and he thought this was the best time to do it.

"They can't treat the little fellow that way," he muttered.

So, Timothy stepped out. "Boo! Boo!" he yelled. And the big brave elephants ran in all directions, leaving Timothy and Dumbo alone.

"Don't be afraid, little fellow," said Timothy Mouse. "I'm your friend. I want to help you. What we have to do is find a use for those ears. They will make you famous. Then, they'll let your mother out of prison, and we'll all live happily ever after."

Dumbo nodded happily. His ears flapped like sails.

"I've got it!" Timothy shouted. "You know the big-elephant balancing act at the end of the show? Well, when they have their pyramid built, you'll jump on the acrobats' springboard and bounce right up to the top of that pyramid, waving a little flag. You'll be the star of the show. Let's sneak out and practice now!"

On their way to the practice field, they passed the prison wagon where Mrs. Jumbo stood, sadly staring out into the night.

How delighted she was to see her baby. And how happy Dumbo was to curl up safe in the curve of his mother's trunk once more.

He told her all about the elephant act, about how unhappy he was without her, and about the wonderful idea Timothy had for making him a success.

Finally, Timothy had to pull Dumbo away, so that they could practice springboard jumping.

When Dumbo could jump from the springboard to a stand twenty feet high, Timothy whispered his idea into the sleeping Ringmaster's ear. And the very next day, as a surprise, Dumbo's jump was added as a highlight to the show.

The great moment came. The pyramid of elephants was swaying in the ring. Dumbo ran down the springboard. Then it happened. He tripped over his flapping ears! Up he bounced in a twirling ball, and he crashed into that great pyramid of elephants, knocking them in every direction at once!

The next day, they made Dumbo into a clown. They painted his face with a foolish grin and dressed him in a baby dress. On his head they put a bonnet. And they used him in the most ridiculous act in the show — a make-believe fire. Dumbo had to jump from the top of a blazing cardboard house, down into the clown-firemen's net. The audience thought it was a great joke. But Dumbo felt terrible. And he was frightened, too.

"Don't worry, Dumbo," Timothy whispered as he curled up in Dumbo's hat brim. "We'll have you starring in the show, yet. You'll be flying high!"

Back in the circus tent, Dumbo fell asleep at once, and he dreamed a beautiful dream. He was the star of a magical circus — a circus the likes of which had never been seen before. In the dream there was a springboard, spotlighted in the center of the tent. Dumbo himself, dressed in a gorgeous costume, stepped onto the springboard, bounced high into the air — and then away he flew.

It seemed as easy as anything and very, very real.

The next morning, Timothy was the first to awaken.
Close beside him, three black crows sat and stared at him.
"What are *you* doing here?" Timothy asked sleepily.
"What are you doing here?" snapped the crows.
At that, Timothy sat up and took another look around
him. "Why — why, where am I?" he gasped. He was still
in the brim of Dumbo's hat, and the hat was still on top of
Dumbo's head. But Dumbo was asleep on the branch of a
tree far, far above the ground!

"How did we get here?" Timothy asked.

"Flew!" the crows cackled.

"Flying?" yelled Timothy. "Dumbo, Dumbo, you flew!"

Slowly Dumbo opened his eyes. He glanced down. He gulped. The he struggled to his feet. He tried to balance in the wobbly tree fork, but he slipped...down, down, down! He bounced from branch to branch, with Timothy clinging on for dear life. *Plonk!* They landed in a brook beneath the tree. The crows chuckled and cawed from above.

Timothy scrambled up out of the water. "Dumbo!" he cried. "You can fly! If you can fly when you're asleep, you can fly when you're awake." So Dumbo tried again…and again….But he could not leave the ground.

With Timothy as his teacher, Dumbo practiced for hours. He ran and he jumped and he hopped — and he tripped. He tried fast and slow takeoffs. He tried standing and running jumps. He counted as he flapped his ears — one, two, three, four. But as hard as he tried, Dumbo could not fly.

At last, the crows felt sorry for him. "Here, try this magic feather," one of them said. "This is how we teach our babies to fly. Hold onto this and you'll be fine."

Dumbo clutched the feather in the tip of his trunk, and he tried once more. The magic-feather trick worked like a charm. No sooner had Dumbo wrapped his trunk around the feather than *flap, flap, flap* went his ears. Up into the air he soared like a bird. He glided, he dipped, and he dived. And he circled over the heads of the cheering crows.

Then he headed back to the circus grounds, with Timothy cheering as loud as he could.

"We must keep your flying a secret — a surprise for this afternoon's show," Timothy decided. So they landed before they reached the tents.

When they got back safely, without being missed, it was time for Dumbo to get into his costume for the big clown act.

Then he had to wait inside the little cardboard house until make-believe fire crackled up around him. But today he did not mind. Because Timothy was with him.

Cr-rr-rr-ack! Cr-rr-ack! crackled the fire. *Clang! Clang!* roared the clown fire engine, rushing toward the blaze.

"Save my baby!" cried a clown, dressed up as a mother.

That was Dumbo's cue to appear at the window. So Timothy tucked the magic feather into the curve of his trunk and climbed up to his place in Dumbo's hat brim.

"Good luck, Dumbo!" he cried.

The firemen brought a big net and held it out.

"Jump, my baby, jump!" shrieked the mother clown.

Dumbo jumped, but as he did, the magic feather slipped and floated away. Now my magic is gone, Dumbo thought.

He plunged down like a stone.

Timothy saw the feather drift past. He knew how Dumbo felt. "It's all right, Dumbo!" he shouted. "The feather was a trick! You can fly by yourself!"

Dumbo heard the shout. Doubtfully, he spread his ears wide. Just two feet above the firemen's net, he stopped his plunge and swooped up into the air!

A mighty gasp arose from the audience. They knew it couldn't be... but it was! Dumbo was flying!

While the crowd roared with delight, Dumbo did power dives, loops, spins, and barrel rolls. He swooped down to pick up peanuts and squirted a trunkful of water on the clowns.

The keepers freed Mrs. Jumbo and brought her to see her baby fly. Now all Dumbo's worries were over.

Soon, Dumbo was a hero from coast to coast. Timothy became his manager and arranged a wonderful contract for Dumbo with a big salary and a pension for his mother.

The circus was renamed Dumbo's Flying Circus, and Dumbo traveled in a special streamlined car.

But best of all, he forgave everyone who had been unkind to him, for his heart was as big as his magical ears.